BON VOYAGE, MR PRESIDENT

AND OTHER STORIES

GABRIEL GARCÍA MÁRQUEZ

BON VOYAGE, MR PRESIDENT

AND OTHER STORIES

Translated by Edith Grossman

penguin books

PENGUIN BOOKS

Published by the Penguin Group
Penguin Books USA Inc., 375 Hudson Street,
New York, New York 10014, U.S.A.
Penguin Books Ltd, 27 Wrights Lane, London W8 5TZ, England
Penguin Books Australia Ltd, Ringwood, Victoria, Australia
Penguin Books Canada Ltd, 10 Alcorn Avenue,
Toronto, Ontario, Canada M4V 3B2
Penguin Books (N.Z.) Ltd, 182–190 Wairau Road,
Auckland 10, New Zealand

Penguin Books Ltd, Registered Offices:
Harmondsworth, Middlesex, England

Published in Penguin Books 1995

These stories are from Gabriel García Márquez's *Strange Pilgrims*,
translated by Edith Grossman, published by Alfred A. Knopf, Inc.
The selections in this volume are reprinted by arrangement with Alfred A.
Knopf, Inc. *Strange Pilgrims* is also published by Penguin Books.
"Bon Voyage, Mr President" first appeared in *The New Yorker*. "Sleeping
Beauty and the Airplane" first appeared in *Playboy*.
Strange Pilgrims was originally published in Spanish as *Doce cuentos peregrinos*
by Mondadori España, S.A., Madrid. Copyright © Gabriel García Márquez,
1992. Copyright © Mondadori España, S.A., 1992.

ISBN 0 14 60.0035 8

Printed in the United States of America

CONTENTS

Bon Voyage, Mr President

He sat on a wooden bench under the yellow leaves in the deserted park, contemplating the dusty swans with both his hands resting on the silver handle of his cane, and thinking about death. On his first visit to Geneva the lake had been calm and clear, and there were tame gulls that would eat out of one's hand, and women for hire who seemed like six-in-the-afternoon phantoms with organdy ruffles and silk parasols. Now the only possible woman he could see was a flower vendor on the deserted pier. It was difficult for him to believe that time could cause so much ruin not only in his life but in the world.

He was one more incognito in the city of illustrious incognitos. He wore the dark blue pin-striped suit, brocade vest, and stiff hat of a retired magistrate. He had the arrogant mustache of a musketeer, abundant blue-black hair with romantic waves, a harpist's hands with the widower's wedding band on his left ring finger, and joyful eyes. Only the weariness of his skin betrayed the state of his health. Even so, at the age of seventy-three, his elegance was still notable. That morning, however, he felt beyond the reach of all vanity. The years of glory and power had been left behind forever, and now only the years of his death remained.

He had returned to Geneva after two world wars, in search of a definitive answer to a pain that the doctors in Martinique could not identify. He had planned on staying no more than two weeks but had spent almost six in exhausting examinations and inconclusive results, and the end was not yet in sight. They looked for the pain in his liver, his kidneys, his pancreas, his prostate, wherever it was not. Until that bitter Thursday, when he had made an appointment for nine in the morning at the neurology department with the least well-known of the many physicians who had seen him.

The office resembled a monk's cell, and the doctor was small and solemn and wore a cast on the broken thumb of his right hand. When the light was turned off, the illuminated X-ray of a spinal column appeared on a screen, but he did not recognize it as his own until the doctor used a pointer to indicate the juncture of two vertebrae below his waist.

'Your pain is here,' he said.

For him it was not so simple. His pain was improbable and devious, and sometimes seemed to be in his ribs on the right side and sometimes in his lower abdomen, and often it caught him off guard with a sudden stab in the groin. The doctor listened to him without moving, the pointer motionless on the screen. 'That is why it eluded us for so long,' he said. 'But now we know it is here.' Then he placed his forefinger on his own temple and stated with precision:

'Although in strictest terms, Mr President, all pain is here.'

His clinical style was so dramatic that the final verdict seemed merciful: the President had to submit to a dangerous and inescapable operation. He asked about the margin of risk, and the old physician enveloped him in an indeterminate light.

'We could not say with certainty,' he answered.

Until a short while before, he explained, the risk of fatal accidents was great, and even more so the danger of different kinds of paralysis of varying degrees. But with the medical advances made during the two wars, such fears were things of the past.

'Don't worry,' the doctor concluded. 'Put your affairs in order and then get in touch with us. But don't forget, the sooner the better.'

It was not a good morning for digesting that piece of bad news, least of all outdoors. He had left the hotel very early, without an overcoat because he saw a brilliant sun through the window, and had walked with measured steps from the Chemin du Beau-Soleil, where the hospital was located, to that refuge for furtive lovers, the Jardin Anglais. He had been there for more than an hour, thinking of nothing but death, when autumn began. The lake became as rough as an angry sea, and an outlaw wind frightened the gulls and made away with the last leaves. The President stood up and, instead of buying a daisy from the flower vendor, he picked one from the public plantings and put it in his buttonhole. She caught him in the act.

'Those flowers don't belong to God, Monsieur,' she said in vexation. 'They're city property.'

He ignored her and walked away with rapid strides, grasping his cane by the middle of the shaft and twirling it from time to time with a rather libertine air. On the Pont du Mont-Blanc the flags of the Confederation, maddened by the sudden gust of wind, were being lowered with as much speed as possible, and the graceful fountain crowned with foam had been turned off earlier than usual. The President did not recognize his usual café on the pier because they had taken down the green awning over the entrance, and the flower-filled terraces of summer had just been closed. Inside the lights burned in the middle of the day, and the string quartet was playing a piece by Mozart full of foreboding. At the counter the President picked up a newspaper from the pile reserved for customers, hung his hat and cane on

3

the rack, put on his gold-rimmed glasses to read at the most isolated table, and only then became aware that autumn had arrived. He began to read the international page, where from time to time he found a rare news item from the Americas, and he continued reading from back to front until the waitress brought him his daily bottle of Evian water. Following his doctors' orders, he had given up the habit of coffee more than thirty years before, but had said, 'If I ever knew for certain that I was going to die, I would drink it again.' Perhaps the time had come.

'Bring me a coffee too,' he ordered in perfect French. And specified without noticing the double meaning, 'Italian-style, strong enough to wake the dead.'

He drank it without sugar, in slow sips, and then turned the cup upside down on the saucer so that the coffee grounds, after so many years, would have time to write out his destiny. The recaptured taste rescued him for an instant from his gloomy thoughts. A moment later, as if it were part of the same sorcery, he sensed someone looking at him. He turned the page with a casual gesture, then glanced over the top of his glasses and saw the pale, unshaven man in a sports cap and a jacket lined with sheepskin, who looked away at once so their eyes would not meet.

His face was familiar. They had passed each other several times in the hospital lobby, he had seen him on occasion riding a motor scooter on the Promenade du Lac while he was contemplating the swans, but he never felt that he had been recognized. He did not, however, discount the idea that this was one of the many persecution fantasies of exile.

He finished the paper at his leisure, floating on the sumptuous
4 cellos of Brahms, until the pain was stronger than the analgesic

of the music. Then he looked at the small gold watch and chain that he carried in his vest pocket and took his two midday tranquilizers with the last swallow of Evian water. Before removing his glasses he deciphered his destiny in the coffee grounds and felt an icy shudder: he saw uncertainty there. At last he paid the bill, left a miser's tip, collected his cane and hat from the rack, and walked out to the street without looking at the man who was looking at him. He moved away with his festive walk, stepping around the beds of flowers devastated by the wind, and thought he was free of the spell. But then he heard steps behind him and came to a halt when he rounded the corner, making a partial turn. The man following him had to stop short to avoid a collision, and his startled eyes looked at him from just a few inches away.

'Señor Presidente,' he murmured.

'Tell the people who pay you not to get their hopes up,' said the President, without losing his smile or the charm of his voice. 'My health is perfect.'

'Nobody knows that better than me,' said the man, crushed by the weight of dignity that had fallen upon him. 'I work at the hospital.'

His diction and cadence, and even his timidity, were raw Caribbean.

'Don't tell me you're a doctor,' said the President.

'I wish I could, Señor. I'm an ambulance driver.'

'I'm sorry,' said the President, convinced of his error. 'That's a hard job.'

'Not as hard as yours, Señor.'

He looked straight at him, leaned on his cane with both hands, and asked with real interest:

'Where are you from?'

'The Caribbean.'

'I already knew that,' said the President. 'But which country?'

'The same as you, Señor,' the man said, and offered his hand. 'My name is Homero Rey.'

The President interrupted him in astonishment, not letting go of his hand.

'Damn,' he said. 'What a fine name!'

Homero relaxed.

'It gets better,' he said. 'Homero Rey de la Casa – I'm Homer King of His House.'

A wintry knife-thrust caught them unprotected in the middle of the street. The President shivered down to his bones and knew that without an overcoat he could not walk the two blocks to the cheap restaurant where he usually ate.

'Have you had lunch?' he asked.

'I never have lunch,' said Homero. 'I eat one meal at night in my house.'

'Make an exception for today,' he said, using all his charm. 'Let me take you to lunch.'

He led him by the arm to the restaurant across the street, its name in gilt on the awning: Le Boeuf Couronné. The interior was narrow and warm, and there seemed to be no empty tables. Homero Rey, surprised that no one recognized the President, walked to the back to request assistance.

'Is he an acting president?' the owner asked.

'No,' said Homero. 'Overthrown.' The owner smiled in approval.

'For them,' he said, 'I always have a special table.'

He led them to an isolated table in the rear of the room, where they could talk as much as they liked. The President thanked him.

'Not everyone recognizes as you do the dignity of exile,' he said.

The specialty of the house was charcoal-broiled ribs of beef. The President and his guest glanced around and saw the great roasted slabs edged in tender fat on the other tables. 'It's magnificent meat,' murmured the President. 'But I'm not allowed to eat it.' He looked at Homero with a roguish eye and changed his tone.

'In fact, I'm not allowed to eat anything.'

'You're not allowed to have coffee either,' said Homero, 'but you drink it anyway.'

'You found that out?' said the President. 'But today was just an exception on an exceptional day.'

Coffee was not the only exception he made that day. He also ordered charcoal-broiled ribs of beef and a fresh vegetable salad with a simple splash of olive oil for dressing. His guest ordered the same, and half a carafe of red wine.

While they were waiting for the meat, Homero took a wallet with no money and many papers out of his jacket pocket, and showed a faded photograph to the President, who recognized himself in shirtsleeves, a few pounds lighter and with intense black hair and mustache, surrounded by a crowd of young men standing on tiptoe to be seen. In a single glance he recognized the place, he recognized the emblems of an abominable election campaign, he recognized the wretched date. 'It's shocking!' he murmured. 'I've always said one ages faster in photographs than in real life.' And he returned the picture with a gesture of finality.

'I remember it very well,' he said. 'It was thousands of years ago, in the cock pit at San Cristóbal de las Casas.'

'That's my town,' said Homero, and he pointed to himself in the group. 'This is me.'

The President recognized him.

'You were a baby!'

'Almost,' said Homero. 'I was with you for the whole southern campaign as a leader of the university brigades.'

The President anticipated his reproach.

'I, of course, did not even notice you,' he said.

'Not at all, you were very nice,' said Homero. 'But there were so many of us there's no way you could remember.'

'And afterward?'

'You know that better than anybody,' said Homero. 'After the military coup, the miracle is that we're both here, ready to eat half a cow. Not many were as lucky.'

Just then their food was brought to the table. The President tied his napkin around his neck, like an infant's bib, and was aware of his guest's silent surprise. 'If I didn't do this I'd ruin a tie at every meal,' he said. Before he began, he tasted the meat for seasoning, approved with a satisfied gesture, and returned to his subject.

'What I can't understand,' he said, 'is why you didn't approach me earlier, instead of tracking me like a bloodhound.'

Homero said that he had recognized him from the time he saw him go into the hospital through a door reserved for very special cases. It was in the middle of summer, and he was wearing a three-piece linen suit from the Antilles, with black-and-white shoes, a daisy in his lapel, and his beautiful hair blowing in the wind. Homero learned that he was alone in Geneva, with no one to help him, for the President knew by heart the city where he had completed his law studies. The hospital administration, at his request, took the internal measures necessary to guarantee his absolute incognito. That very night Homero and his wife agreed to communicate with him. And yet for five weeks he had followed him, waiting for a propitious moment, and perhaps would not have been capable of speaking if the President had not confronted him.

'I'm glad I did, although the truth is, it doesn't bother me at all to be alone.'

'It's not right.'

'Why?' asked the President with sincerity. 'The greatest victory of my life has been having everyone forget me.'

'We remember you more than you imagine,' said Homero, not hiding his emotion. 'It's a joy to see you like this, young and healthy.'

'And yet,' he said without melodrama, 'everything indicates that I'll die very soon.'

'Your chances of recovery are very good,' said Homero.

The President gave a start of surprise but did not lose his sense of humor.

'Damn!' he exclaimed. 'Has medical confidentiality been abolished in beautiful Switzerland?'

'There are no secrets for an ambulance driver in any hospital anywhere in the world,' said Homero.

'Well, what I know I found out just two hours ago from the lips of the only man who could have known it.'

'In any case, you will not have died in vain,' said Homero. 'Someone will restore you to your rightful place as a great example of honor.'

The President feigned a comic astonishment.

'Thank you for warning me,' he said.

He ate as he did everything: without haste and with great care. As he did so he looked Homero straight in the eye, and the younger man had the impression he could see what the older man was thinking. After a long conversation filled with nostalgic evocations, the President's smile turned mischievous.

'I had decided not to worry about my corpse,' he said, 'but now I see that I must take precautions worthy of a detective novel to keep it hidden.'

'It won't do any good,' Homero joked in turn. 'In the hospital no mystery lasts longer than an hour.'

When they had finished their coffee, the President read the bottom of his cup, and again he shuddered: the message was the same. Still, his expression did not change. He paid the bill in cash but first checked the total several times, counted his money several times with excessive care, and left a tip that merited no more than a grunt from the waiter.

'It has been a pleasure,' he concluded as he took his leave of Homero. 'I haven't set a date yet for the surgery, and I haven't even decided if I'm going to have it done or not. But if all goes well, we'll see each other again.'

'And why not before?' said Homero. 'Lázara, my wife, does cooking for rich people. Nobody makes shrimp and rice better than she does, and we'd like to invite you to our house some night soon.'

'I'm not allowed to have shellfish, but I'll be happy to eat it,' he said. 'Just tell me when.'

'Thursday is my day off,' said Homero.

'Perfect,' said the President. 'Thursday at seven I'll be at your house. It will be a pleasure.'

'I'll come by for you,' said Homero. 'Hôtellerie Dames, Fourteen Rue de l'Industrie. Behind the station. Is that right?'

'That's right,' said the President, and he stood up, more charming than ever. 'It appears you even know my shoe size.'

'Of course, Señor,' said Homero with amusement. 'Size forty-one.'

What Homero Rey did not tell the President, but did tell for years afterward to anyone willing to listen, was that his original intention was not so innocent. Like other ambulance drivers, he had made certain arrangements with funeral parlors and insurance companies to sell their services inside the hospital, above all to foreign patients of limited means. The profits were small and had to be shared with other employees who passed around the confidential files of patients with serious illnesses. But it was some consolation for an exile with no future who just managed to support his wife and two children on a ridiculous salary.

Lázara Davis, his wife, was more realistic. A slender mulatta from San Juan, Puerto Rico, she was small and solid, the color of cooked caramel, and had the eyes of a vixen, which matched her temperament very well. They had met in the charity ward of the hospital, where she worked as a general aide after a financier from her country, who had brought her to Geneva as a nurse-maid, left her adrift in the city. She and Homero had been married in a Catholic ceremony, although she was a Yoruban princess, and they lived in a two-bedroom apartment on the eighth floor of a building that had no elevator and was occupied by African émigrés. Their daughter, Bárbara, was nine years old, and their son, Lázaro, who was seven, showed signs of slight mental retardation.

Lázara Davis was intelligent and evil-tempered, but she had a tender heart. She considered herself a pure Taurus and believed with blind faith in her astral portents. Yet she had never been able to realize her dream of earning a living as an astrologer to 11 millionaires. On the other hand, she made occasional and sometimes significant contributions to the family's finances by preparing dinners for wealthy matrons who impressed their guests by making them believe they had cooked the exciting Antillean dishes themselves. Homero's timidity was painful, and he had no ambitions beyond the little he earned, but Lázara could not conceive of life without him because of the innocence of his heart and the caliber of his member. Things had gone well for them, but each year was more difficult and the children were growing. At the time of the President's arrival they had begun dipping into their savings of five years. And so when Homero Rey discovered him among the incognito patients in the hospital, their hopes were raised.

They did not know with precision what they were going to ask for, or with what right. At first they planned to sell him the complete funeral, including embalming and repatriation. But little by little they realized that his death did not seem quite as imminent as it had at the beginning. On the day of the lunch they were confused by doubts.

The truth is that Homero had not been a leader of the university brigades or of anything else, and the only part he ever played in the election campaign was to be included in the photograph that they managed to find as if by miracle under a pile of papers in the closet. But his fervor was true. It was also true that he had been obliged to flee the country because of his participation in street protests against the military coup, although his only reason for still living in Geneva after so many years was his poverty of spirit. And so one lie more or less should not have been an obstacle to gaining the President's favor.

The first surprise for both of them was that the illustrious exile lived in a fourth-class hotel in the sad district of Les

Grottes, among Asian émigrés and ladies of the night, and ate alone in cheap restaurants, when Geneva was filled with suitable residences for politicians in disgrace. Day after day, Homero had seen him repeat that day's actions. He had accompanied him with his eyes, sometimes at a less than prudent distance, in his nocturnal strolls among the mournful walls and tattered yellow bell-flowers of the old city. He had seen him lost in thought for hours in front of the statue of Calvin. Breathless with the ardent perfume of the jasmines, he had followed him step by step up the stone staircase to contemplate the slow summer twilights from the top of the Bourg-de-Four. One night he saw him in the first rain of the season, without an overcoat or an umbrella, standing in line with the students for a Rubinstein concert. 'I don't know why he didn't catch pneumonia,' Homero said afterward to his wife. On the previous Saturday, when the weather began to change, he had seen him buy an autumn coat with a fake mink collar, not in the glittering shops along the Rue du Rhône, where fugitive emirs made their purchases, but in the flea market.

'Then there's nothing we can do!' exclaimed Lázara when Homero told her about it. 'He's a damn miser who'll give himself a charity funeral and be buried in a pauper's grave. We'll never get anything out of him.'

'Maybe he's really poor,' said Homero, 'after so many years out of work.'

'Oh, baby, it's one thing to be a Pisces with an ascendant Pisces, and another thing to be a damn fool,' said Lázara. 'Everybody knows he made off with the country's gold and is the richest exile in Martinique.'

Homero, who was ten years her senior, had grown up influenced by news articles to the effect that the President had 13 studied in Geneva and supported himself by working as a construction laborer. Lázara, on the other hand, had been raised among the scandals in the opposition press, which were magnified in the opposition household where she had been a nursemaid from the time she was a girl. As a consequence, on the night Homero came home breathless with jubilation because he had eaten lunch with the President, she was not convinced by the argument that he had taken him to an expensive restaurant. It annoyed her that Homero had not asked for any of the countless things they had dreamed of, from scholarships for the children to a better job at the hospital. The President's decision to leave his body for the vultures instead of spending his francs on a suitable burial and a glorious repatriation seemed to confirm her suspicions. But the final straw was the news Homero saved for last, that he had invited the President for a meal of shrimp and rice on Thursday night.

'That's just what we needed,' shouted Lázara, 'to have him die here, poisoned by canned shrimp, and have to use the children's savings to bury him.'

In the end, what determined her behavior was the weight of her conjugal loyalty. She had to borrow three silver place settings and a crystal salad bowl from one neighbor, an electric coffeepot from another, and an embroidered tablecloth and a china coffee service from a third. She took down the old curtains and put up the new ones, used only on holidays, and removed the covers from the furniture. She spent an entire day scrubbing the floors, shaking out dust, shifting things around, until she achieved just the opposite of what would have benefited them most, which was to move their guest with the respectability of their poverty.

On Thursday night, when he had caught his breath after

climbing to the eighth floor, the President appeared at the door with his new old coat and melon-shaped hat from another time, and a single rose for Lázara. She was impressed by his virile good looks and his manners worthy of a prince, but beyond all that she saw what she had expected to see: a false and rapacious man. She thought him impertinent, because she had cooked with the windows open to keep the smell of shrimp from filling the house, and the first thing he did when he entered was to take a deep breath, as if in sudden ecstasy, and exclaim with eyes closed and arms spread wide, 'Ah, the smell of our ocean!' She thought him stingier than ever for bringing her just one rose, stolen no doubt from the public gardens. She thought him insolent for the disdain with which he looked at the newspaper clippings of his presidential glories, and the pennants and flags of the campaign, which Homero had pinned with so much candor to the living room wall. She thought him hard hearted, because he did not even greet Bárbara and Lázaro, who had made a gift for him, and in the course of the dinner he referred to two things he could not abide: dogs and children. She hated him. Nevertheless, her Caribbean sense of hospitality overcame her prejudices. She had put on the African gown she wore on special occasions, and her *santería* beads and bracelets, and during the meal she did not make any unnecessary gestures or say a single superfluous word. She was more than irreproachable: she was perfect.

The truth was that shrimp and rice was not one of the accomplishments of her kitchen, but she prepared it with the best will, and it turned out very well. The President took two helpings and showed no restraint in his praise, and he was delighted by the slices of fried ripe plantain and the avocado salad, although he did not share in their nostalgia. Lázara resigned herself to just listening until dessert, when for no apparent reason Homero became trapped in the dead-end street of the existence of God.

'I do believe God exists,' said the President, 'but has nothing to do with human beings. He's involved in much bigger things.'

'I only believe in the stars,' said Lázara, and she scrutinized the President's reaction. 'What day were you born?'

'The eleventh of March.'

'I knew it,' said Lázara with a triumphant little start, and asked in a pleasant voice, 'Don't you think two Pisces at the same table are too many?'

The men were still discussing God when she went to the kitchen to prepare coffee. She had cleared the table, and longed with all her heart for the evening to end well. On her way back to the living room with the coffee, she was met with a passing remark of the President's, which astounded her.

'Have no doubt, my dear friend: it would be the worst thing that could happen to our poor country if I were president.'

Homero saw Lázara in the doorway with the borrowed china cups and coffeepot and thought she was going to faint. The President also took notice. 'Don't look at me like that, Señora,' he said in an amiable tone. 'I'm speaking from the heart.' And then, turning to Homero, he concluded:

'It's just as well I'm paying a high price for my foolishness.'

Lázara served the coffee and turned off the light above the table because its harsh illumination was not conducive to conversation, and the room was left in intimate shadow. For the first time she became interested in the guest, whose wit could not hide his sadness. Lázara's curiosity increased when he finished his coffee and turned the cup upside down in the saucer so the grounds could settle.

The President told them he had chosen the island of Martinique for his exile because of his friendship with the poet Aimé Césaire, who at that time had just published his *Cahier d'un retour au pays natal,* and had helped him begin a new life. With what remained of his wife's inheritance, the President bought a house made of noble wood in the hills of Fort-de-France, with screens at the windows and a terrace overlooking the sea and filled with primitive flowers, where it was a pleasure to sleep with the sound of crickets and the molasses-and-rum breeze from the sugar mills. There he stayed with his wife, fourteen years older than he and an invalid since the birth of their only child, fortified against fate by his habitual rereading of the Latin classics, in Latin, and by the conviction that this was the final act of his life. For years he had to resist the temptation of all kinds of adventures proposed to him by his defeated partisans.

'But I never opened another letter again,' he said. 'Never, once I discovered that even the most urgent were less urgent after a week, and that in two months one forgot about them and the person who wrote them.'

He looked at Lázara in the semi-darkness when she lit a cigarette, and took it from her with an avid movement of his fingers. After a long drag, he held the smoke in his throat. Startled, Lázara picked up the pack and the box of matches to light another, but he returned the burning cigarette to her. 'You smoke with so much pleasure I could not resist,' he said. Then he had to release the smoke because he began to cough.

'I gave up the habit many years ago, but it never gave me up altogether,' he said. 'On occasion it has defeated me. Like now.'

The cough jolted him two more times. The pain returned. The President checked his small pocket watch and took his two evening pills. Then he peered into the bottom of his cup: nothing had changed, but this time he did not shudder.

'Some of my old supporters have been presidents after me,' he said.

'Sáyago,' said Homero.

'Sáyago and others,' he said. 'All of us usurping an honor we did not deserve with an office we did not know how to fill. Some pursue only power, but most are looking for even less: a job.'

Lázara became angry.

'Do you know what they say about you?' she asked.

Homero intervened in alarm:

'They're lies.'

'They're lies and they're not lies,' said the President with celestial calm. 'When it has to do with a president, the worst ignominies may be both true and false at the same time.'

He had lived in Martinique all the days of his exile, his only contact with the outside world the few news items in the official paper. He had supported himself teaching classes in Spanish and Latin at an official *lycée*, and with the translations that Aimé Césaire commissioned from time to time. The heat in August was unbearable, and he would stay in the hammock until noon, reading to the hum of the fan in his bedroom. Even at the hottest times of the day his wife tended to the birds she raised in freedom outdoors, protecting herself from the sun with a broad-brimmed straw hat adorned with artificial fruit and organdy flowers. But when the temperature fell, it was good to sit in the cool air on the terrace, he with his eyes fixed on the ocean until it grew dark, and she in her wicker rocking chair, wearing the torn hat, and rings with bright stones on every finger, watching the ships of the world pass by. 'That one's bound for Puerto Santo,' she would say. 'That one almost can't move, it's so loaded down with bananas from Puerto Santo,' she would say. For it did not seem possible to her that any ship could pass by that was not from their country. He pretended not to hear, although in the long run she managed to forget better than he because she lost her memory. They would sit this way until the clamorous twilights came to an end and they had to take refuge in the house, defeated by the mosquitoes. During one of those many Augusts, as he was reading the paper on the terrace, the President gave a start of surprise.

'I'll be damned,' he said. 'I've died in Estoril!'

His wife, adrift in her drowsiness, was horrified by the news. The article consisted of six lines on the fifth page of the newspaper printed just around the corner, in which his occasional translations were published and whose manager came to visit him from time to time. And now it said that he had died in Estoril de Lisboa, the resort and refuge of European decadence, where he had never been and which was, perhaps, the only place in the world where he would not have wanted to die. His wife did die, in fact, a year later, tormented by the last memory left to her: the recollection of her only child, who had taken part in the overthrow of his father and was later shot by his own accomplices.

The President sighed. 'That's how we are, and nothing can save us,' he said. 'A continent conceived by the scum of the earth without a moment of love: the children of abductions, rapes, violations, infamous dealings, deceptions, the union of enemies with enemies.' He faced Lázara's African eyes, which scrutinized him without pity, and tried to win her over with the eloquence of an old master.

'Mixing the races means mixing tears with spilled blood. What can one expect from such a potion?'

19

Lázara fixed him to his place with the silence of death. But she gained control of herself a little before midnight and said good-bye to him with a formal kiss. The President refused to allow Homero to accompany him to the hotel, although he could not stop him from helping him find a taxi. When Homero came back, his wife was raging with fury.

'That's one president in the world who really deserved to be overthrown,' she said. 'What a son of a bitch.'

Despite Homero's efforts to calm her, they spent a terrible, sleepless night. Lázara admitted that he was one of the best-looking men she had ever seen, with a devastating seductive power and a stud's virility. 'Just as he is now, old and fucked up, he must still be a tiger in bed,' she said. But she thought he had squandered these gifts of God in the service of pretense. She could not bear his boasts that he had been his country's worst president. Or his ascetic airs, when, she was convinced, he owned half the sugar plantations in Martinique. Or the hypocrisy of his contempt for power, when it was obvious he would give anything to return to the presidency long enough to make his enemies bite the dust.

'And all of that,' she concluded, 'just to have us worshipping at his feet.'

'What good would that do him?' asked Homero.

'None at all,' she said. 'But the fact is that being seductive is an addiction that can never be satisfied.'

Her rage was so great that Homero could not bear to be with her in bed, and he spent the rest of the night wrapped in a blanket on the sofa in the living room. Lázara also got up in the middle of the night, naked from head to toe – her habitual state when she slept or was at home – and talked to herself in a monologue on only one theme. In a single stroke she erased from human memory all traces of the hateful supper. At daybreak she returned what she had borrowed, replaced the new curtains with the old, and put the furniture back where it belonged so that the house was as poor and decent as it had been until the night before. Then she tore down the press clippings, the portraits, the banners and flags from the abominable campaign, and threw them all in the trash with a final shout.

'You can go to hell!'

A week after the dinner, Homero found the President waiting for him as he left the hospital, with the request that he accompany him to his hotel. They climbed three flights of steep stairs to a garret that had a single skylight looking out on an ashen sky; clothes were drying on a line stretched across the room. There was also a double bed that took up half the space, a hard chair, a washstand and a portable bidet, and a poor man's armoire with a clouded mirror. The President noted Homero's reaction.

'This is the burrow I lived in when I was a student,' he said as if in apology. 'I made the reservation from Fort-de-France.'

From a velvet bag he removed and displayed on the bed the last remnants of his wealth: several gold bracelets adorned with a variety of precious stones, a three-strand pearl necklace, and two others of gold and precious stones; three gold chains with saints' medals; a pair of gold and emerald earrings, another of gold and diamonds, and a third of gold and rubies; two reliquaries and a locket; eleven rings with all kinds of precious settings; and a diamond tiara worthy of a queen. From a case he took out three pairs of silver cuff links and two of gold, all with matching tie clips, and a pocket watch plated in white gold. Then he removed his six decorations from a shoe box: two of gold, one of silver, and the rest of no value.

'It's all I have left in life,' he said.

He had no alternative but to sell it all to meet his medical expenses, and he asked Homero to please do that for him with the greatest discretion. But Homero did not feel he could oblige if he did not have the proper receipts.

The President explained that they were his wife's jewels, a legacy from a grandmother who had lived in colonial times and had inherited a packet of shares in Colombian gold mines. The watch, the cuff links and tie clips were his. The decorations, of course, had not belonged to anyone before him.

'I don't believe anybody has receipts for these kinds of things,' he said.

Homero was adamant.

'In that case,' the President reflected, 'there's nothing I can do but take care of it myself.'

He began to gather up the jewelry with calculated calm. 'I beg you to forgive me, my dear Homero, but there is no poverty worse than that of an impoverished president,' he said. 'Even surviving seems contemptible.' At that moment Homero saw him with his heart and laid down his weapons.

Lázara came home late that night. From the door she saw the jewels glittering on the table under the mercurial light, and it was as if she had seen a scorpion in her bed.

'Don't be an idiot, baby,' she said, frightened. 'Why are those things here?'

Homero's explanation disturbed her even more. She sat down to examine the pieces, one by one, with all the care of a gold-
22 smith. At a certain point she sighed and said, 'They must be

worth a fortune.' At last she sat looking at Homero and could find no way out of her dilemma.

'Damn it,' she said. 'How can we know if everything that man says is true?'

'Why shouldn't it be?' said Homero. 'I've just seen that he washes his own clothes and dries them on a line in his room, just like we do.'

'Because he's cheap,' said Lázara.

'Or poor,' said Homero.

Lázara examined the jewels again, but now with less attention because she too had been conquered. And so the next morning she put on her best clothes, adorned herself with the pieces that seemed most expensive, wore as many rings as she could on every finger, even her thumb, and all the bracelets that would fit on each arm, and went out to sell them. 'Let's see if anyone asks Lázara Davis for receipts,' she said as she left, strutting with laughter. She chose just the right jewelry store, one with more pretensions than prestige, where she knew they bought and sold without asking too many questions, and she walked in terrified but with a firm step.

A thin, pale salesman in evening dress made a theatrical bow as he kissed her hand and asked how he could help her. Because of the mirrors and intense lights the interior was brighter than the day, and the entire shop seemed made of diamonds. Lázara, almost without looking at the clerk for fear he would see through the farce, followed him to the rear of the store.

He invited her to sit at one of three Louis XV escritoires that served as individual counters, and over it he spread an immaculate cloth. Then he sat across from Lázara and waited.

'How may I help you?'

She removed the rings, the bracelets, the necklaces, the earrings, everything that she was wearing in plain view, and began to place them on the escritoire in a chessboard pattern. All she wanted, she said, was to know their true value.

The jeweler put a glass up to his left eye and began to examine the pieces in clinical silence. After a long while, without interrupting his examination, he asked:

'Where are you from?'

Lázara had not anticipated that question.

'Ay, Señor,' she sighed, 'very far away.'

'I can imagine,' he said.

He was silent again, while Lázara's terrible golden eyes scrutinized him without mercy. The jeweler devoted special attention to the diamond tiara and set it apart from the other jewelry. Lázara sighed.

'You are a perfect Virgo,' she said.

The jeweler did not interrupt his examination.

'How do you know?'

'From the way you behave,' said Lázara.

He made no comment until he had finished, and he addressed her with the same circumspection he had used at the beginning.

'Where does all this come from?'

'It's a legacy from my grandmother,' said Lázara in a tense voice. 'She died last year in Paramaribo, at the age of ninety-seven.'

The jeweler looked into her eyes. 'I'm very sorry,' he said. 'But their only value is the weight of the gold.' He picked up the tiara with his fingertips and made it sparkle under the dazzling light.

24 'Except for this,' he said. 'It is very old, Egyptian perhaps,

and would be priceless if it were not for the poor condition of the diamonds. In any case it has a certain historical value.'

But the stones in the other treasures, the amethysts, emeralds, rubies, opals – all of them, without exception – were fake. 'No doubt the originals were good,' said the jeweler as he gathered up the pieces to return them to her. 'But they have passed so often from one generation to another that the legitimate stones have been lost along the way and been replaced by bottle glass.' Lázara felt a green nausea, took a deep breath, and controlled her panic. The salesman consoled her:

'It often happens, Madame.'

'I know,' said Lázara, relieved. 'That's why I want to get rid of them.'

She felt then that she was beyond the farce, and became herself again. With no further delay she took the cuff links, the pocket watch, the tie clips, the decorations of gold and silver, and the rest of the President's personal trinkets out of her handbag and placed them all on the table.

'This too?' asked the jeweler.

'All of it,' said Lázara.

She was paid in Swiss francs that were so new she was afraid her fingers would be stained with fresh ink. She accepted the bills without counting them, and the jeweler's leave-taking at the door was as ceremonious as his greeting. As he held the glass door open for her, he stopped her for a moment.

'And one final thing, Madame,' he said. 'I'm an Aquarius.'

Early that evening Homero and Lázara took the money to the hotel. After further calculations, they found that a little more money was still needed. And so the President began removing and placing on the bed his wedding ring, his watch and chain, and the cuff links and tie clip he was wearing.

Lázara handed back the ring.

'Not this,' she said. 'A keepsake like this can't be sold.'

The President acknowledged what she said and put the ring back on his finger. Lázara also returned the watch and chain. 'Not this either,' she said. The President did not agree, but she put him in his place.

'Who'd even try to sell a watch in Switzerland?'

'We already did,' said the President.

'Yes, but not the watch. We sold the gold.'

'This is gold too,' said the President.

'Yes,' said Lázara. 'You may get by without surgery, but you have to know what time it is.'

She would not take his gold-rimmed eyeglasses either, although he had another pair with tortoiseshell frames. She hefted the pieces in her hand, and put an end to all his doubts.

'Besides,' she said, 'this will be enough.'

Before she left she took down his damp clothes, without consulting him, to dry and iron them at home. They rode on the motor scooter, Homero driving and Lázara sitting behind him, her arms around his waist. The street-lights had just turned on in the mauve twilight. The wind had blown away the last leaves, and the trees looked like plucked fossils. A tow truck drove along the Rhone, its radio playing at full volume and leaving a stream of music along the streets. Georges Brassens was singing: *Mon amour tiens bien la barre, le temps va passer par là, et le temps est un barbare dans le genre d'Attila; par là où son cheval passe l'amour ne repousse pas.* Homero and Lázara rode in silence, intoxicated by the song and the remembered scent of hyacinth. After a while, she seemed to awaken from a long sleep.

'Damn it,' she said.

'What?'

'The poor old man,' said Lázara. 'What a shitty life!'

On the following Friday, the seventh of October, the President underwent five hours of surgery that, for the moment, left matters as obscure as they had been before. In the strictest sense, the only consolation was knowing he was alive. After ten days he was moved to a room with other patients, and Homero and Lázara could visit him. He was another man: disoriented and emaciated, his sparse hair fell out at a touch of the pillow. All that was left of his former presence was the fluid grace of his hands. His first attempt at walking with two orthopedic canes was heartbreaking. Lázara stayed and slept at his bedside to save him the expense of a private nurse. One of the other patients in the room spent the first night screaming with his terror of dying. Those endless nights did away with Lázara's last reservations.

Four months after his arrival in Geneva, he was discharged from the hospital. Homero, a meticulous administrator of the President's scant funds, paid the hospital bill and took him home in his ambulance with other employees who helped carry him to the eighth floor. They put him in the bedroom of the children he never really acknowledged, and little by little he returned to reality. He devoted himself to his rehabilitative exercises with military rigor, and walked again with just his cane. But even in his good clothes from the old days, he was far from being the same man in either appearance or behavior. Fearing the winter that promised to be very severe, and which in fact turned out to be the harshest of the century, he decided, against the advice of 27 his doctors, who wanted to keep him under observation for a while longer, to return home on a ship leaving Marseilles on December 13. At the last minute he did not have enough money for his passage, and without telling her husband Lázara tried to make up the difference with one more scraping from her children's savings, but there too she found less than she expected. Then Homero confessed that without telling her he had used it to finish paying the hospital bill.

'Well,' Lázara said in resignation. 'Let's say he's our oldest son.'

On December 11 they put him on the train to Marseilles in a heavy snowstorm, and it was not until they came home that they found a farewell letter on the children's night table, where he also left his wedding ring for Bárbara, along with his dead wife's wedding band, which he had never tried to sell, and the watch and chain for Lázaro. Since it was a Sunday, some Caribbean neighbors who had learned the secret came to the Cornavin Station with a harp band from Veracruz. The President was gasping for breath in his raffish overcoat and a long multi-colored scarf that had belonged to Lázara, but even so he stood in the open area of the last car and waved goodbye with his hat in the lashing wind. The train was beginning to accelerate when Homero realized he still had his cane. He ran to the end of the platform and threw it hard enough for the President to catch, but it fell under the wheels and was destroyed. It was a moment of horror. The last thing Lázara saw was the President's trembling hand stretching to grasp the cane and never reaching it, and the conductor who managed to grab the snow-covered old man by his scarf and save him in midair. Lázara ran in utter terror to her husband, trying to laugh behind her tears.

'My God,' she shouted, 'nothing can kill that man.'

He arrived home safe and sound, according to his long telegram of thanks. Nothing more was heard from him for over a year. At last they received a six-page hand-written letter in which it was impossible to recognize him. The pain had returned, as intense and punctual as before, but he had resolved to ignore it and live life as it came. The poet Aimé Césaire had given him another cane, with mother-of-pearl inlay, but he had decided not to use it. For six months he had been eating meat and all kinds of shellfish, and could drink up to twenty cups a day of the bitterest coffee. But he had stopped reading the bottom of the cup, because the predictions never came true. On the day he turned seventy-five, he drank a few glasses of exquisite Martinique rum, which agreed with him, and began to smoke again. He did not feel better, of course, but neither did he feel worse. Nevertheless, the real reason for the letter was to tell them that he felt tempted to return to his country as the leader of a reform movement – a just cause for the honor of the nation – even if he gained only the poor glory of not dying of old age in his bed. In that sense, the letter ended, his trip to Geneva had been providential.

June 1979

Sleeping Beauty and the Airplane

She was beautiful and lithe, with soft skin the color of bread and
eyes like green almonds, and she had straight black hair that
reached to her shoulders, and an aura of antiquity that could just
as well have been Indonesian as Andean. She was dressed with
subtle taste: a lynx jacket, a raw silk blouse with very delicate
flowers, natural linen trousers, and shoes with a narrow stripe
the color of bougainvillea. 'This is the most beautiful woman
I've ever seen,' I thought when I saw her pass by with the
stealthy stride of a lioness while I waited in the check-in line at
Charles de Gaulle Airport in Paris for the plane to New York.
She was a supernatural apparition who existed only for a moment
and disappeared into the crowd in the terminal.

It was nine in the morning. It had been snowing all night, and
traffic was heavier than usual in the city streets, and even slower
on the highway, where trailer trucks were lined up on the
shoulder and automobiles steamed in the snow. Inside the airport
terminal, however, it was still spring.

I stood behind an old Dutch woman who spent almost an
hour arguing about the weight of her eleven suitcases. I was
beginning to feel bored when I saw the momentary apparition
who left me breathless, and so I never knew how the dispute
ended. Then the ticket clerk brought me down from the clouds
with a reproach for my distraction. By way of an excuse, I asked
her if she believed in love at first sight. 'Of course,' she said.
'The other kinds are impossible.' She kept her eyes fixed on the
computer screen and asked whether I preferred a seat in smoking

30

or non-smoking.

'It doesn't matter,' I said with intentional malice, 'as long as I'm not beside the eleven suitcases.'

She expressed her appreciation with a commercial smile but did not look away from the glowing screen.

'Choose a number,' she told me: 'Three, four, or seven.'

'Four.'

Her smile flashed in triumph.

'In the fifteen years I've worked here,' she said, 'you're the first person who hasn't chosen seven.'

She wrote the seat number on my boarding pass and returned it with the rest of my papers, looking at me for the first time with grape-colored eyes that were a consolation until I could see Beauty again. Only then did she inform me that the airport had just been closed and all flights delayed.

'For how long?'

'That's up to God,' she said with her smile. 'The radio said this morning it would be the biggest snow-storm of the year.'

She was wrong: it was the biggest of the century. But in the first-class waiting room, spring was so real that there were live roses in the vases and even the canned music seemed as sublime and tranquilizing as its creators had intended. All at once it occurred to me that this was a suitable shelter for Beauty, and I looked for her in the other waiting areas, staggered by my own boldness. But most of the people were men from real life who read newspapers in English while their wives thought about someone else as they looked through the panoramic windows at the planes dead in the snow, the glacial factories, the vast fields of Roissy devastated by fierce lions. By noon there was no place to sit, and the heat had become so unbearable that I escaped for a breath of air.

Outside I saw an overwhelming sight. All kinds of people had crowded into the waiting rooms and were camped in the stifling corridors and even on the stairways, stretched out on the floor with their animals, their children, and their travel gear. Communication with the city had also been interrupted, and the palace of transparent plastic resembled an immense space capsule stranded in the storm. I could not help thinking that Beauty too must be somewhere in the middle of those tamed hordes, and the fantasy inspired me with new courage to wait.

By lunchtime we had realized that we were shipwrecked. The lines were interminable outside the seven restaurants, the cafeterias, the packed bars, and in less than three hours they all had to be closed because there was nothing left to eat or drink. The children, who for a moment seemed to be all the children in the world, started to cry at the same time, and a herd smell began to rise from the crowd. It was a time for instinct. In all that scrambling, the only thing I could find to eat were the last two cups of vanilla ice cream in a children's shop. The waiters were putting chairs on tables as the patrons left, while I ate very slowly at the counter, seeing myself in the mirror with the last little cardboard cup and the last little cardboard spoon, and thinking about Beauty.

The flight to New York, scheduled for eleven in the morning, left at eight that night. By the time I managed to board, the other first-class passengers were already in their seats, and a flight attendant led me to mine. My heart stopped. In the seat next to mine, beside the window, Beauty was taking possession of her space with the mastery of an expert traveler. 'If I ever wrote this, nobody would believe me,' I thought. And I just managed to stammer an indecisive greeting that she did not hear.

She settled in as if she were going to live there for many years, putting each thing in its proper place and order, until her seat was arranged like the ideal house, where everything was within reach. In the meantime, a steward brought us our welcoming champagne. I took a glass to offer to her, but thought better of it just in time. For she wanted only a glass of water, and she asked the steward, first in incomprehensible French and then in an English only somewhat more fluent, not to wake her for any reason during the flight. Her warm, serious voice was tinged with Oriental sadness.

When he brought the water, she placed a cosmetics case with copper corners, like a grandmother's trunk, on her lap, and took two golden pills from a box that contained others of various colors. She did everything in a methodical, solemn way, as if nothing unforeseen had happened to her since her birth. At last she pulled down the shade on the window, lowered the back of her seat as far as it would go, covered herself to the waist with a blanket without taking off her shoes, put on a sleeping mask, turned her back to me, and then slept without a single pause, without a sigh, without the slightest change in position, for the eight eternal hours and twelve extra minutes of the flight to New York.

It was an ardent journey. I have always believed that there is nothing more beautiful in nature than a beautiful woman, and it was impossible for me to escape even for a moment from the spell of that storybook creature who slept at my side. The steward disappeared as soon as we took off and was replaced by a Cartesian attendant who tried to awaken Beauty to hand her a toiletry case and a set of earphones for listening to music. I repeated the instructions she had given the steward, but the attendant insisted on hearing from Beauty's own lips that she did not want supper either. The steward had to confirm her 33 instructions, and even so he reproached me because Beauty had not hung the little cardboard 'Do Not Disturb' sign around her neck.

I ate a solitary supper, telling myself in silence everything I would have told her if she had been awake. Her sleep was so steady that at one point I had the distressing thought that the pills she had taken were not for sleeping but for dying. With each drink I raised my glass and toasted her.

'To your health, Beauty.'

When supper was over the lights were dimmed and a movie was shown to no one, and the two of us were alone in the darkness of the world. The biggest storm of the century had ended, and the Atlantic night was immense and limpid, and the plane seemed motionless among the stars. Then I contemplated her, inch by inch, for several hours, and the only sign of life I could detect were the shadows of the dreams that passed along her forehead like clouds over water. Around her neck she wore a chain so fine it was almost invisible against her golden skin, her perfect ears were unpierced, her nails were rosy with good health, and on her left hand was a plain band. Since she looked no older than twenty, I consoled myself with the idea that it was not a wedding ring but the sign of an ephemeral engagement. 'To know you are sleeping, certain, secure, faithful channel of renunciation, pure line, so close to my manacled arms,' I thought on the foaming crest of champagne, repeating the masterful sonnet by Gerardo Diego. Then I lowered the back of my seat to the level of hers, and we lay together, closer than if we had been in a marriage bed. The climate of her breathing was the same as that of her voice, and her skin exhaled a delicate breath that could only be the scent of her beauty. It seemed incredible: the previous spring I had read a beautiful novel by Yasunari Kawabata about the ancient bourgeois of Kyoto who paid enormous sums to spend the night watching the most beautiful girls in the city, naked and drugged, while they agonized with love in the same bed. They could not wake them, or touch them, and they did not even try, because the essence of their pleasure was to see them sleeping. That night, as I watched over Beauty's sleep, I not only understood that senile refinement but lived it to the full.

'Who would have thought,' I said to myself, my vanity exacerbated by champagne, 'that I'd become an ancient Japanese at this late date.'

I think I slept several hours, conquered by champagne and the mute explosions of the movie, and when I awoke my head was splitting. I went to the bathroom. Two seats behind mine the old woman with the eleven suitcases lay in an awkward sprawl, like a forgotten corpse on a battlefield. Her reading glasses, on a chain of colored beads, were on the floor in the middle of the aisle, and for a moment I enjoyed the malicious pleasure of not picking them up.

After I got rid of the excesses of champagne, I caught sight of myself, contemptible and ugly, in the mirror, and was amazed that the devastation of love could be so terrible. The plane lost altitude without warning, then managed to straighten out and continue full speed ahead. The 'Return to Your Seat' sign went on. I hurried out with the hope that God's turbulence might awaken Beauty and she would have to take refuge in my arms to escape her terror. In my haste I almost stepped on the Dutch woman's glasses and would have been happy if I had. But I retraced my steps, picked them up, and put them on her lap in sudden gratitude for her not having chosen seat number four before I did.

Beauty's sleep was invincible. When the plane stabilized, I had to resist the temptation to shake her on some pretext, because all I wanted in the last hour of the flight was to see her awake, even if she were furious, so that I could recover my freedom, and perhaps my youth. But I couldn't do it. 'Damn it,' I said to myself with great scorn. 'Why wasn't I born a Taurus!'

She awoke by herself at the moment the landing lights went on, and she was as beautiful and refreshed as if she had slept in a rose garden. That was when I realized that, like old married couples, people who sit next to each other on airplanes do not say good morning to each other when they wake up. Nor did she. She took off her mask, opened her radiant eyes, straightened the back of the seat, moved the blanket aside, shook her hair that fell into place of its own weight, put the toiletry case back on her knees, and applied rapid, unnecessary make-up, which took just enough time so that she did not look at me until the plane door opened. Then she put on her lynx jacket, almost stepped over me with a conventional excuse in pure Latin American Spanish, left without even saying good-bye or at least thanking me for all I had done to make our night together a happy one, and disappeared into the sun of today in the Amazon jungle of New York.

June 1982

'I Only Came to Use the Phone'

One rainy spring afternoon, while María de la Luz Cervantes was driving alone back to Barcelona, her rented car broke down in the Monegros desert. She was twenty-seven years old, a thoughtful, pretty Mexican who had enjoyed a certain fame as a music-hall performer a few years earlier. She was married to a cabaret magician, whom she was to meet later that day after visiting some relatives in Zaragoza. For an hour she made desperate signals to the cars and trucks that sped past her in the storm, until at last the driver of a ramshackle bus took pity on her. He did warn her, however, that he was not going very far.

'It doesn't matter,' said María. 'All I need is a telephone.'

That was true, and she needed it only to let her husband know that she would not be home before seven. Wearing a student's coat and beach shoes in April, she looked like a bedraggled little bird, and she was so distraught after her mishap that she forgot to take the car keys. A woman with a military air was sitting next to the driver, and she gave María a towel and a blanket and made room for her on the seat. María wiped off the worst of the rain and then sat down, wrapped herself in the blanket, and tried to light a cigarette, but her matches were wet. The woman sharing the seat gave her a light and asked for one of the few cigarettes that were still dry. While they smoked, María gave in to a desire to vent her feelings and raised her voice over the noise of the rain and the clatter of the bus. The woman interrupted her by placing a forefinger to her lips.

'They're asleep,' she whispered.

María looked over her shoulder and saw that the bus was full of women of uncertain ages and varying conditions who were sleeping in blankets just like hers. Their serenity was contagious, and María curled up in her seat and succumbed to the sound of the rain. When she awoke, it was dark and the storm had dissolved into an icy drizzle. She had no idea how long she had slept or what place in the world they had come to. Her neighbor looked watchful.

'Where are we?' María asked.

'We've arrived,' answered the woman.

The bus was entering the cobbled courtyard of an enormous, gloomy building that seemed to be an old convent in a forest of colossal trees. The passengers, just visible in the dim light of a lamp in the courtyard, sat motionless until the woman with the military air ordered them out of the bus with the kind of primitive directions used in nursery school. They were all older women, and their movements were so lethargic in the half-light of the courtyard that they looked like images in a dream. María, the last to climb down, thought they were nuns. She was less certain when she saw several women in uniform who received them at the door of the bus, pulled the blankets over their heads to keep them dry, and lined them up single file, directing them not by speaking but with rhythmic, peremptory clapping. María said good-bye and tried to give the blanket to the woman whose seat she had shared, but the woman told her to use it to cover her head while she crossed the courtyard and then return it at the porter's office.

'Is there a telephone?' María asked.

'Of course,' said the woman. 'They'll show you where it is.'

She asked for another cigarette, and María gave her the rest of the damp pack. 'They'll dry on the way,' she said. The woman waved good-bye from the running board, and called 'Good luck' in a voice that was almost a shout. The bus pulled away without giving her time to say anything else.

María started running toward the doorway of the building. A matron tried to stop her with an energetic clap of the hands, but had to resort to an imperious shout: 'Stop, I said!' María looked out from under the blanket and saw a pair of icy eyes and an inescapable forefinger pointing her into the line. She obeyed. Once inside the vestibule she separated from the group and asked the porter where the telephone was. One of the matrons returned her to the line with little pats on the shoulder while she said in a saccharine voice:

'This way, beautiful, the telephone's this way.'

María walked with the other women down a dim corridor until they came to a communal dormitory, where the matrons collected the blankets and began to assign beds. Another matron, who seemed more humane and of higher rank to María, walked down the line comparing a list of names with those written on cardboard tags stitched to the bodices of the new arrivals. When she reached María, she was surprised to see that she was not wearing her identification.

'I only came to use the phone,' María told her.

She explained with great urgency that her car had broken down on the highway. Her husband, who performed magic tricks at parties, was waiting for her in Barcelona because they had three engagements before midnight, and she wanted to let him know she would not be there in time to go with him. It was almost seven o'clock. He had to leave home in ten minutes, and she was afraid he would cancel everything because she was late. The matron appeared to listen to her with attention.

'What's your name?' she asked.

María said her name with a sigh of relief, but the woman did not find it after going over the list several times. With some alarm she questioned another matron, who had nothing to say and shrugged her shoulders.

'But I only came to use the phone,' said María.

'Sure, honey,' the supervisor told her, escorting her to her bed with a sweetness that was too patent to be real, 'if you're good you can call anybody you want. But not now, tomorrow.'

Then something clicked in María's mind, and she understood why the women on the bus moved as if they were on the bottom of an aquarium. They were, in fact, sedated with tranquilizers, and that dark palace with the thick stone walls and frozen stairways was really a hospital for female mental patients. She raced out of the dormitory in dismay, but before she could reach the main door a gigantic matron wearing mechanic's coveralls stopped her with a blow of her huge hand and held her immobile on the floor in an armlock. María, paralyzed with terror, looked at her sideways.

'For the love of God,' she said. 'I swear by my dead mother I only came to use the phone.'

Just one glance at her face was enough for María to know that no amount of pleading would move that maniac in coveralls who was called Herculina because of her uncommon strength. She was in charge of difficult cases, and two inmates had been strangled to death by her polar bear arm skilled in the art of killing by mistake. It was established that the first case had been an accident. The second proved less clear, and Herculina was admonished and warned that the next time she would be subjected to a thorough investigation. The accepted story was that this black sheep of a fine old family had a dubious history of suspicious accidents in various mental hospitals throughout Spain.

They had to inject María with a sedative to make her sleep the first night. When a longing to smoke roused her before dawn, she was tied to the metal bars of the bed by her wrists and ankles. She shouted, but no one came. In the morning, while her husband could find no trace of her in Barcelona, she had to be taken to the infirmary, for they found her senseless in a swamp of her own misery.

When she regained consciousness she did not know how much time had passed. But now the world seemed a haven of love. Beside her bed, a monumental old man with a flatfooted walk and a calming smile gave her back her joy in being alive with two masterful passes of his hand. He was the director of the sanatorium.

Before saying anything to him, without even greeting him, María asked for a cigarette. He lit one and handed it to her, along with the pack, which was almost full. María could not hold back her tears.

'Now is the time to cry to your heart's content,' the doctor said in a soporific voice. 'Tears are the best medicine.'

María unburdened herself without shame, as she had never been able to do with her casual lovers in the empty times that followed lovemaking. As he listened, the doctor smoothed her hair with his fingers, arranged her pillow to ease her breathing, guided her through the labyrinth of her uncertainty with a wisdom and a sweetness she never had dreamed possible. This was, for the first time in her life, the miracle of being understood by a man who listened to her with all his heart and did not expect to go to bed with her as a reward. At the end of a long hour, when she had bared the depths of her soul, she asked permission to speak to her husband on the telephone.

The doctor stood up with all the majesty of his position. 'Not yet, princess,' he said, patting her cheek with more tenderness than she ever had felt before. 'Everything in due course.' He gave her a bishop's blessing from the door, asked her to trust him, and disappeared forever.

That same afternoon María was admitted to the asylum with a serial number and a few superficial comments concerning the enigma of where she had come from and the doubts surrounding her identity. In the margin the director had written an assessment in his own hand: *agitated*.

Just as María had foreseen, her husband left their modest apartment in the Horta district half an hour behind schedule for his three engagements. It was the first time she had been late in the almost two years of their free and very harmonious union, and he assumed it was due to the heavy downpours that had devastated the entire province that weekend. Before he went out he pinned a note to the door with his itinerary for the night.

At the first party, where all the children were dressed in kangaroo costumes, he omitted his best illusion, the invisible fish, because he could not do it without her assistance. His second engagement was in the house of a ninety-three-year-old woman in a wheelchair, who prided herself on having celebrated each of her last thirty birthdays with a different magician. He was so troubled by María's absence that he could not concentrate on the simplest tricks. At his third engagement, the one he did every night at a café on the Ramblas, he gave an uninspired performance for a group of French tourists who could not believe what they saw because they refused to believe in magic. After each show he telephoned his house, and waited in despair for María to answer. After the last call he could no longer control his concern that something had happened to her.

On his way home, in the van adapted for public performances, he saw the splendor of spring in the palm trees along the Paseo de Gracia, and he shuddered at the ominous thought of what the city would be like without María. His last hope vanished when he found his note still pinned to the door. He was so troubled he forgot to feed the cat.

I realize now as I write this that I never learned his real name, because in Barcelona we knew him only by his professional name: Saturno the Magician. He was a man of odd character and irredeemable social awkwardness, but María had more than enough of the tact and charm he lacked. It was she who led him by the hand through this community of great mysteries, where no man would have dreamed of calling after midnight to look for his wife. Saturno had, soon after he arrived, and he preferred to forget the incident. And so that night he settled for calling Zaragoza, where a sleepy grandmother told him with no alarm that María had said goodbye after lunch. He slept for just an hour at dawn. He had a muddled dream in which he saw María wearing a ragged wedding dress spattered with blood, and he woke with the fearful certainty that this time she had left him forever, to face the vast world without him.

She had deserted three different men, including him, in the last five years. She had left him in Mexico City six months after they met, when they were in the throes of pleasure from their demented lovemaking in a maid's room in the Anzures district. One morning, after a night of unspeakable profligacy, María was gone. She left behind everything that was hers, even the ring from her previous marriage, along with a letter in which she said she was incapable of surviving the torment of that wild love. Saturno thought she had returned to her first husband, a high school classmate she had married in secret while still a minor 43 and abandoned for another man after two loveless years. But no: she had gone to her parents' house, and Saturno followed to get her back regardless of the cost. His pleading was unconditional, he made many more promises than he was prepared to keep, but he came up against an invincible determination. 'There are short loves and there are long ones,' she told him. And she concluded with a merciless, 'This was a short one.' Her inflexibility forced him to admit defeat. But in the early hours of the morning of All Saints' Day, when he returned to his orphan's room after almost a year of deliberate forgetting, he found her asleep on the living room sofa with the crown of orange blossoms and long tulle train worn by virgin brides.

María told him the truth. Her new fiancé, a childless widower with a settled life and a mind to marry forever in the Catholic Church, had left her dressed and waiting at the altar. Her parents decided to hold the reception anyway, and she played along with them. She danced, sang with the mariachis, had too much to drink, and in a terrible state of belated remorse left at midnight to find Saturno.

He was not home, but she found the keys in the flower pot in the hall, where they always hid them. Now she was the one whose surrender was unconditional. 'How long this time?' he asked. She answered with a line by Vinicius de Moraes: 'Love is eternal for as long as it lasts.' Two years later, it was still eternal.

María seemed to mature. She renounced her dreams of being an actress and dedicated herself to him, both in work and in bed. At the end of the previous year they had attended a magicians' convention in Perpignan, and on their way home they visited Barcelona for the first time. They liked it so much they had been living here for eight months, and it suited them so well they bought an apartment in the very Catalonian neighborhood of

Horta. It was noisy, and they had no porter, but there was more than enough room for five children. Their happiness was all one could hope for, until the weekend when she rented a car and went to visit her relatives in Zaragoza, promising to be back by seven on Monday night. By dawn on Thursday there was still no word from her.

On Monday of the following week, the insurance company for the rented car called and asked for María. 'I don't know anything,' said Saturno. 'Look for her in Zaragoza.' He hung up. A week later a police officer came to the house to report that the car had been found, stripped bare, on a back road to Cádiz, nine hundred kilometers from the spot where María had abandoned it. The officer wanted to know if she had further details regarding the theft. Saturno was feeding the cat, and he did not look up when he told him straight out that the police shouldn't waste their time because his wife had left him and he didn't know where she had gone or with whom. His conviction was so great that the officer felt uncomfortable and apologized for his questions. They declared the case closed.

The suspicion that María might leave him again had assailed Saturno at Easter in Cadaqués, where Rosa Regás had invited them to go sailing. In the Marítim, the crowded, sordid bar of the *gauche divine* during the twilight of Francoism, twenty of us were squeezed together around one of those wrought-iron tables that had room only for six. After she smoked her second pack of cigarettes of the day, María ran out of matches. A thin, downy arm wearing a Roman bronze bracelet made its way through the noisy crowd at the table and gave her a light. She said thank you without looking at the person she was thanking, but Saturno the Magician saw him – a bony, clean-shaven adolescent as pale as death, with a very black ponytail that hung down to his waist. 45

The windowpanes in the bar just managed to withstand the fury of the spring tramontana wind, but he wore a kind of street pajama made of raw cotton, and a pair of farmer's sandals.

They did not see him again until late autumn, in a sea-food bar in La Barceloneta, wearing the same plain cotton outfit and a long braid instead of the ponytail. He greeted them both as if they were old friends, and the way he kissed María, and the way she kissed him back, struck Saturno with the suspicion that they had been seeing each other in secret. Days later he happened to come across a new name and phone number that María had written in their household address book, and the unmerciful lucidity of jealousy revealed to him whose they were. The intruder's background was the final proof: he was twenty-two years old, the only child of a wealthy family, and a decorator of fashionable shop windows, with a casual reputation as a bisexual and a well-founded notoriety as a paid comforter of married women. But Saturno managed to restrain himself until the night María did not come home. Then he began calling him every day, from six in the morning until just before the following dawn, every two or three hours at first, and then whenever he was near a telephone. The fact that no one answered intensified Saturno's martyrdom.

On the fourth day an Andalusian woman who was there just to clean picked up the phone. 'The gentleman's gone away,' she said, with enough vagueness to drive him mad. Saturno did not resist the temptation of asking if Señorita María was in by any chance.

'Nobody named María lives here,' the woman told him. 'The gentleman is a bachelor.'

'I know,' he said. 'She doesn't live there, but sometimes she visits, right?'

The woman became annoyed.

'Who the hell is this, anyway?'

Saturno hung up. The woman's denial seemed one more confirmation of what for him was no longer a suspicion but a burning certainty. He lost control. In the days that followed he called everyone he knew in Barcelona, in alphabetical order. No one could tell him anything, but each call deepened his misery, because his jealous frenzies had become famous among the unrepentant night owls of the *gauche divine* and they responded with any kind of joke that would make him suffer. Only then did he realize how alone he was in that beautiful, lunatic, impenetrable city, where he would never be happy. At dawn, after he fed the cat, he hardened his heart to keep from dying and resolved to forget María.

After two months María had not yet adjusted to life in the sanatorium. She survived by just picking at the prison rations with flatware chained to the long table of unfinished wood, her eyes fixed on the lithograph of General Francisco Franco that presided over the gloomy medieval dining room. At first she resisted the canonical hours with their mindless routine of matins, lauds, vespers, as well as the other church services that took up most of the time. She refused to play ball in the recreation yard, or to make artificial flowers in the workshop that a group of inmates attended with frenetic diligence. But after the third week she began, little by little, to join in the life of the cloister. After all, said the doctors, every one of them started out the same way, and sooner or later they became integrated into the community.

The lack of cigarettes, resolved in the first few days by a matron who sold them for the price of gold, returned to torment her again when she had spent the little money she had with her. 47

Then she took comfort in the newspaper cigarettes that some inmates made with the butts they picked out of the trash, for her obsessive desire to smoke had become as intense as her fixation on the telephone. Later on, the few pesetas she earned making artificial flowers allowed her an ephemeral consolation.

Hardest of all was her loneliness at night. Many inmates lay awake in the semi-darkness, as she did, not daring to do anything because the night matron at the heavy door secured with a chain and padlock was awake too. One night, however, overcome with grief, María asked in a voice loud enough for the woman in the next bed to hear:

'Where are we?'

The grave, lucid voice of her neighbor answered:

'In the pit of hell.'

'They say this is the country of the Moors,' said another, distant voice that resounded throughout the dormitory. 'And it must be true, because in the summer, when there's a moon, you can hear the dogs barking at the sea.'

The chain running through the locks sounded like the anchor of a galleon, and the door opened. Their pitiless guardian, the only creature who seemed alive in the instantaneous silence, began walking from one end of the dormitory to the other. María was seized with terror, and only she knew why.

Since her first week in the sanatorium, the night matron had been proposing outright that María sleep with her in the guard-room. She began in a concrete, businesslike tone: an exchange of love for cigarettes, for chocolate, for whatever she wanted. 'You'll have everything,' the matron said, tremulous. 'You'll be the queen.' When María refused, she changed her tactics, leaving little love notes under her pillow, in the pockets of her robe, in the most unexpected places. They were messages of a heartbreaking urgency that could have moved a stone. On the night of the dormitory incident, it had been more than a month that she had seemed resigned to defeat.

When she was certain the other inmates were asleep, the matron approached María's bed and whispered all kinds of tender obscenities in her ear while she kissed her face, her neck tensed with terror, her rigid arms, her exhausted legs. Then, thinking perhaps that María's paralysis stemmed not from fear but from compliance, she dared to go further. That was when María hit her with the back of her hand and sent her crashing into the next bed. The enraged matron stood up in the midst of the uproar created by the agitated inmates.

'You bitch!' she shouted. 'We'll rot together in this hellhole until you go crazy for me.'

Summer arrived without warning on the first Sunday in June, requiring emergency measures because during Mass the sweltering inmates began taking off their shapeless serge gowns. With some amusement María watched the spectacle of naked patients being chased like blind chickens up and down the aisles by the matrons. In the confusion she tried to protect herself from wild blows, and she somehow found herself alone in an empty office, where the incessant ring of a telephone had a pleading tone. María answered without thinking and heard a distant, smiling voice that took great pleasure in imitating the telephone company's time service:

'The time is forty-five hours, ninety-two minutes, and one hundred seven seconds.'

'Asshole,' said María.

She hung up, amused. She was about to leave when she realized she was allowing a unique opportunity to slip away. She dialed six digits, with so much tension and so much haste she   49 was not sure it was her home number. She waited, her heart racing, she heard the avid, sad sound of the familiar ring, once, twice, three times, and at last she heard the voice of the man she loved, in the house without her.

'Hello?'

She had to wait for the knot of tears that formed in her throat to dissolve.

'Baby, sweetheart,' she sighed.

Her tears overcame her. On the other end of the line there was a brief, horrified silence, and a voice burning with jealousy spit out the word:

'Whore!'

And he slammed down the receiver.

That night, in an attack of rage, María pulled down the lithograph of the Generalissimo in the refectory, crashed it with all her strength into the stained-glass window that led to the garden, and threw herself to the floor, covered in blood. She still had enough fury left to resist the blows of the matrons who tried, with no success, to restrain her, until she saw Herculina standing in the doorway with her arms folded, staring at her. María gave up. Nevertheless, they dragged her to the ward for violent patients, subdued her with a hose spurting icy water, and injected turpentine into her legs. The swelling that resulted prevented her from walking, and María realized there was nothing in the world she would not do to escape that hell. The following week, when she was back in the dormitory, she tiptoed to the night matron's room and knocked at the door.

María's price, which she demanded in advance, was that the matron send a message to her husband. The matron agreed, on the condition that their dealings be kept an absolute secret. And 50 she pointed an inexorable forefinger at her.

'If they ever find out, you die.'

And so, on the following Saturday, Saturno the Magician drove to the asylum for women in the circus van, which he had prepared to celebrate María's return. The director himself received him in his office, which was as clean and well ordered as a battleship, and made an affectionate report on his wife's condition. No one had known where she came from, or how or when, since the first information regarding her arrival was the official admittance form he had dictated after interviewing her. An investigation begun that same day had proved inconclusive. In any event, what most intrigued the director was how Saturno had learned his wife's whereabouts. Saturno protected the matron.

'The insurance company told me,' he said.

The director nodded, satisfied. 'I don't know how insurance companies manage to find out everything,' he said. He looked over the file lying on his ascetic's desk, and concluded:

'The only certainty is the seriousness of her condition.'

He was prepared to authorize a visit with all the necessary precautions if Saturno the Magician would promise, for the good of his wife, to adhere without question to the rules of behavior that he would indicate. Above all with reference to how he treated her, in order to avoid a recurrence of the fits of rage that were becoming more and more frequent and dangerous.

'How strange,' said Saturno. 'She always was quick-tempered, but had a lot of self-control.'

The doctor made a learned man's gesture. 'There are behaviors that remain latent for many years, and then one day they erupt,' he said. 'All in all, it is fortunate she happened to come here, because we specialize in cases requiring a firm hand.' Then he warned him about María's strange obsession with the telephone. 51

'Humor her,' he said.

'Don't worry, Doctor,' Saturno said with a cheerful air. 'That's my specialty.'

The visiting room, a combination of prison cell and confessional, was the former locutory of the convent. Saturno's entrance was not the explosion of joy they both might have expected. María stood in the middle of the room, next to a small table with two chairs and a vase empty of flowers. It was obvious she was ready to leave, with her lamentable strawberry-colored coat and a pair of disreputable shoes given to her out of charity. Herculina stood in a corner, almost invisible, her arms folded. María did not move when she saw her husband come in, and her face, still marked by the shattered window glass, showed no emotion. They exchanged routine kisses.

'How do you feel?' he asked her.

'Happy you're here at last, baby,' she said. 'This has been death.'

They did not have time to sit down. Drowning in tears, María told him about the miseries of the cloister, the brutality of the matrons, the food not fit for dogs, the endless nights when terror kept her from closing her eyes.

'I don't even know how many days I've been here, or how many months or years, all I know is that each one has been worse than the last,' and she sighed with all her soul. 'I don't think I'll ever be the same.'

'That's all over now,' he said caressing the recent scars on her face with his fingertips. 'I'll come every Saturday. More often than that, if the director lets me. You'll see, everything will turn out just fine.'

She fixed her terrified eyes on his. Saturno tried to use his performer's charm. He told her, in the puerile tone of all great lies, a sweetened version of the doctor's prognosis. 'It means,' he concluded, 'that you still need a few more days to make a complete recovery.' María understood the truth.

'For God's sake, baby,' she said, stunned. 'Don't tell me you think I'm crazy too!'

'The things you think of!' he said, trying to laugh. 'But it really will be much better for everybody if you stay here a while. Under better conditions, of course.'

'But I've already told you I only came to use the phone!' said María.

He did not know how to react to her dreadful obsession. He looked at Herculina. She took advantage of the opportunity to point at her wristwatch as a sign that it was time to end the visit. María intercepted the signal, glanced behind her, and saw Herculina tensing for an imminent attack. Then she clung to her husband's neck, screaming like a real madwoman. He freed himself with as much love as he could muster, and left her to the mercies of Herculina, who jumped her from behind. Without giving María time to react, she applied an armlock with her left hand, put her other iron arm around her throat, and shouted at Saturno the Magician:

'Leave!'

Saturno fled in terror.

But on the following Saturday, when he had recovered from the shock of the visit, he returned to the sanatorium with the cat, which he had dressed in an outfit identical to his: the red-and-yellow tights of the great Leotardo, a top hat, and a swirling cape that seemed made for flying. He drove the circus van into the courtyard of the cloister, and there he put on a prodigious show lasting almost three hours, which the inmates enjoyed from the balconies with discordant shouts and inopportune applause. 53

They were all there except María, who not only refused to receive her husband but would not even watch him from the balconies. Saturno felt wounded to the quick.

'It is a typical reaction,' the director consoled him. 'It will pass.'

But it never passed. After attempting many times to see María again, Saturno did all he could to have her accept a letter from him, but to no avail. She returned it four times, unopened and with no comments. Saturno gave up but continued leaving a supply of cigarettes at the porter's office without ever finding out if they reached María, until at last reality defeated him.

No one heard any more about him except that he married again and returned to his own country. Before leaving Barcelona he gave the half-starved cat to a casual girlfriend, who also promised to take cigarettes to María. But she disappeared too. Rosa Regás remembered seeing her in the Corte Inglés department store about twelve years ago, with the shaved head and orange robes of some Oriental sect, and very pregnant. She told Rosa she had taken cigarettes to María as often as she could, and settled some unforeseen emergencies for her, until one day she found only the ruins of the hospital, which had been demolished like a bad memory of those wretched times. María seemed very lucid on her last visit, a little overweight, and content with the peace of the cloister. That was the day she also brought María the cat, because she had spent all the money that Saturno had given her for its food.

April 1978

Light is Like Water

At Christmas the boys asked again for a rowboat.

'Okay,' said their papa, 'we'll buy it when we get back to Cartagena.'

Totó, who was nine years old, and Joel, who was seven, were more determined than their parents believed.

'No,' they said in chorus. 'We need it here and now.'

'To begin with,' said their mother, 'the only navigable water here is what comes out of the shower.'

She and her husband were both right. Their house in Cartagena de Indias had a yard with a dock on the bay, and a shed that could hold two large yachts. Here in Madrid, on the other hand, they were crowded into a fifth-floor apartment at 47 Paseo de la Castellana. But in the end neither of them could refuse because they had promised the children a rowboat complete with sextant and compass if they won their class prizes in elementary school, and they had. And so their papa bought everything and said nothing to his wife, who was more reluctant than he to pay gambling debts. It was a beautiful aluminum boat with a gold stripe at the waterline.

'The boat's in the garage,' their papa announced at lunch. 'The problem is, there's no way to bring it up in the elevator or by the stairs, and there's no more space available in the garage.'

On the following Saturday afternoon, however, the boys invited their classmates to help bring the boat up the stairs, and they managed to carry it as far as the maid's room.

'Congratulations,' said their papa. 'Now what?'

'Now nothing,' said the boys. 'All we wanted was to have the boat in the room, and now it's there.'

On Wednesday night, as they did every Wednesday, the parents went to the movies. The boys, lords and masters of the house, closed the doors and windows and broke the glowing bulb in one of the living-room lamps. A jet of golden light as cool as water began to pour out of the broken bulb, and they let it run to a depth of almost three feet. Then they turned off the electricity, took out the rowboat, and navigated at will among the islands in the house.

This fabulous adventure was the result of a frivolous remark I made while taking part in a seminar on the poetry of household objects. Totó asked me why the light went on with just the touch of a switch, and I did not have the courage to think about it twice.

'Light is like water,' I answered. 'You turn the tap and out it comes.'

And so they continued sailing every Wednesday night, learning how to use the sextant and the compass, until their parents came home from the movies and found them sleeping like angels on dry land. Months later, longing to go farther, they asked for complete skin-diving outfits: masks, fins, tanks, and compressed-air rifles.

'It's bad enough you've put a rowboat you can't use in the maid's room,' said their father. 'To make it even worse, now you want diving equipment too.'

'What if we win the Gold Gardenia Prize for the first semester?' said Joel.

'No,' said their mother in alarm. 'That's enough.'

Their father reproached her for being intransigent.

'These kids don't win so much as a nail when it comes to

doing what they're supposed to,' she said, 'but to get what they want they're capable of taking it all, even the teacher's chair.'

In the end the parents did not say yes or no. But in July, Totó and Joel each won a Gold Gardenia and the public recognition of the headmaster. That same afternoon, without having to ask again, they found the diving outfits in their original packing in their bedroom. And so the following Wednesday, while their parents were at the movies seeing *Last Tango in Paris*, they filled the apartment to a depth of two fathoms, dove like tame sharks under the furniture, including the beds, and salvaged from the bottom of the light things that had been lost in darkness for years.

At the end-of-the-year awards ceremony, the brothers were acclaimed as examples for the entire school and received certificates of excellence. This time they did not have to ask for anything because their parents asked them what they wanted. They were so reasonable that all they wanted was a party at home as a treat for their classmates.

Their papa, when he was alone with his wife, was radiant.

'It's a proof of their maturity,' he said.

'From your lips to God's ear,' said their mother.

The following Wednesday, while their parents were watching *The Battle of Algiers*, people walking along the Paseo de la Castellana saw a cascade of light falling from an old building hidden among the trees. It spilled over the balconies, poured in torrents down the façade, and rushed along the great avenue in a golden flood that lit the city all the way to the Guadarrama.

In response to the emergency, firemen forced the door on the fifth floor and found the apartment brimming with light all the way to the ceiling. The sofa and easy chairs covered in leopard skin were floating at different levels in the living-room, among the bottles from the bar and the grand piano with its Manila shawl that fluttered half submerged like a golden manta ray. Household objects, in the fullness of their poetry, flew with their own wings through the kitchen sky. The marching-band instruments that the children used for dancing drifted among the bright-colored fish freed from their mother's aquarium, which were the only creatures alive and happy in the vast illuminated marsh. Everyone's toothbrush floated in the bathroom, along with Papa's condoms and Mama's jars of creams and her spare bridge, and the television set from the master bedroom floated on its side, still tuned to the final episode of the midnight movie for adults only.

At the end of the hall, moving with the current and clutching the oars, with his mask on and only enough air to reach port, Totó sat in the stern of the boat, searching for the lighthouse, and Joel, floating in the prow, still looked for the north star with the sextant, and floating through the entire house were their thirty-seven classmates, eternalized in the moment of peeing into the pot of geraniums, singing the school song with the words changed to make fun of the headmaster, sneaking a glass of brandy from Papa's bottle. For they had turned on so many lights at the same time that the apartment had flooded, and two entire classes at the elementary school of Saint Julian the Hospitaler drowned on the fifth floor of 47 Paseo de la Castellana. In Madrid, Spain, a remote city of burning summers and icy winds, with no ocean or river, whose landbound indigenous population had never mastered the science of navigating on light.

December 1978